THE TALE OF
MRS. TIGGY-WINKLE

BY BEATRIX POTTER

FREDERICK WARNE

ONCE upon a time there was a little girl called Lucie, who lived at a farm called Little-town. She was a good little girl—only she was always losing her pocket-handkerchiefs! One day little Lucie came into the farm-yard crying—oh, she did cry so! "I've lost my pocket-handkin! Three handkins and a pinny! Have *you* seen them, Tabby Kitten?"

THE kitten went on washing her white paws; so Lucie asked a speckled hen—

"Sally Henny-penny, have *you* found three pocket-handkins?"

But the speckled hen ran into a barn, clucking— "I go barefoot, barefoot, barefoot!"

AND then Lucie asked Cock Robin sitting on a twig.

Cock Robin looked sideways at Lucie with his bright black eye, and he flew over a stile and away.

Lucie climbed upon the stile and looked up at the hill behind Little-town—a hill that goes up—up—into the clouds as though it had no top!

And a great way up the hill-side she thought she saw some white things spread upon the grass.

Lucie scrambled up the hill as fast as her short legs would carry her; she ran along a steep path-way—up and up—until Little-town was right away down below—she could have dropped a pebble down the chimney!

PRESENTLY she
came to a spring,
bubbling out from
the hill-side.

Some one had stood a
tin can upon a stone to
catch the water— but
the water was already
running over, for the
can was no bigger than an egg-cup! And where
the sand upon the path was wet— there were
foot-marks of a *very* small person.

Lucie ran on, and on.

The path ended under a big rock. The grass
was short and green, and there were clothes-
props cut from bracken stems, with lines of
plaited rushes, and a heap of tiny clothes pins—
but no pocket-handkerchiefs!

BUT there was something else—a door!
straight into the hill; and inside it some one
was singing—

"Lily-white and clean, oh!
With little frills between, oh!
Smooth and hot—red rusty spot
Never here be seen, oh!"

LUCIE knocked—once—twice, and
interrupted the song. A little frightened voice
called out "Who's that?"

Lucie opened the door: and what do you think
there was inside the hill?—a nice clean kitchen
with a flagged floor and wooden beams—just
like any other farm kitchen. Only the ceiling
was so low that
Lucie's head
nearly touched
it; and the
pots and
pans were
small, and
so was
everything
there.

THERE was a nice hot singey smell; and at the table, with an iron in her hand, stood a very stout short person staring anxiously at Lucie.

Her print gown was tucked up, and she was wearing a large apron over her striped petticoat. Her little black nose went sniffle, sniffle, snuffle, and her eyes went twinkle, twinkle; and underneath her cap—where Lucie had yellow curls—that little person had PRICKLES!

"WHO are you?" said Lucie. "Have you seen my pocket-handkins?"

The little person made a bob-curtsey—"Oh, yes, if you please'm; my name is Mrs. Tiggy-winkle; oh, yes if you please'm, I'm an excellent clear-starcher!" And she took something out of a clothes-basket, and spread it on the ironing-blanket.

"WHAT'S that thing?"
said Lucie—"that's not
my pocket-handkin?"

"Oh no, if you please'm;
that's a little scarlet
waist-coat belonging
to Cock Robin!"

And she ironed it and
folded it, and put it
on one side.

Then she took
something else off
a clothes-horse—

"That isn't my
pinny?" said Lucie.

"Oh no, if you please'm;
that's a damask table-cloth belonging to Jenny
Wren; look how it's stained with currant wine!
It's very bad to wash!" said Mrs. Tiggy-winkle.

MRS. TIGGY-WINKLE'S nose went sniffle, sniffle, snuffle, and her eyes went twinkle, twinkle; and she fetched another hot iron from the fire.

"THERE'S one of my pocket-handkins!" cried
Lucie—"and there's my pinny!"

Mrs. Tiggy-winkle ironed it, and goffered it,
and shook out the frills.

"Oh that *is* lovely!" said Lucie.

"AND what are those long yellow things with fingers like gloves?"

"Oh, that's a pair of stockings belonging to Sally Henny-penny—look how she's worn the heels out with scratching in the yard! She'll very soon go barefoot!" said Mrs. Tiggy-winkle.

"Why, there's another handkersniff—but it isn't mine; it's red?"

"Oh no, if you please'm; that one belongs to old Mrs. Rabbit; and it *did* so smell of onions! I've had to wash it separately, I can't get out the smell."

"There's another one of mine," said Lucie.

"WHAT are those funny little white things?"

"That's a pair of mittens belonging to Tabby Kitten; I only have to iron them; she washes them herself."

"There's my last pocket-handkin!" said Lucie.

"AND what are you dipping into the basin of starch?"

"They're little dicky shirt-fronts belonging to Tom Tit-mouse—most terrible particular!" said Mrs. Tiggy-winkle.

"Now I've finished my ironing; I'm going to air some clothes."

"WHAT are these dear soft fluffy things?" said Lucie.

"Oh those are woolly coats belonging to the little lambs at Skelghyl."

"Will their jackets take off?" asked Lucie.

"Oh yes, if you please'm; look at the sheep-mark on the shoulder. And here's one marked for Gatesgarth, and three that come from Little-town. They're *always* marked at washing!" said Mrs. Tiggy-winkle.

AND she hung up all sorts and sizes of
clothes—small brown coats of mice; and one
velvety black moleskin waist-coat; and a red
tail-coat with no tail belonging to Squirrel
Nutkin; and a very much shrunk blue jacket
belonging to Peter Rabbit; and a petticoat, not
marked, that had gone lost in the washing—and
at last the basket was empty!

THEN Mrs. Tiggy-winkle made tea—a cup
for herself and a cup for Lucie. They sat before
the fire on a bench and looked sideways at one
another. Mrs. Tiggy-winkle's hand, holding
the tea-cup, was very very brown, and very very
wrinkly with the soap-suds; and all through
her gown and her cap,
there were *hair-
pins* sticking
wrong end out;
so that Lucie
didn't like to
sit too near her.

When they had finished tea, they tied up
the clothes in bundles; and Lucie's pocket-
handkerchiefs were folded up inside her clean
pinny, and fastened with a silver safety-pin.

And then they made up the fire with turf, and
came out and locked the door, and hid the key
under the door-sill.

THEN away down the hill trotted Lucie and
Mrs. Tiggy-winkle with the bundles of clothes!
All the way down the path little animals came
out of the fern to meet them; the very first
that they met were Peter Rabbit and Benjamin
Bunny!

AND she gave them their nice clean clothes; and all the little animals and birds were so very much obliged to dear Mrs. Tiggy-winkle.

So that at the bottom of the hill when they came to the stile, there was nothing left to carry except Lucie's one little bundle.

LUCIE scrambled up the stile with the bundle in her hand; and then she turned to say "Good-night," and to thank the washer-woman—But what a *very* odd thing! Mrs. Tiggy-winkle had not waited either for thanks or for the washing bill!

She was running running running up the hill —and where was her white frilled cap? and her shawl? and her gown—and her petticoat?

AND *how* small she had grown—and *how* brown—and covered with PRICKLES!

Why! Mrs. Tiggy-winkle was nothing but a HEDGEHOG.

(Now some people say that little Lucie had been asleep upon the stile—but then how could she have found three clean pocket-handkins and a pinny, pinned with a silver safety-pin?

And besides—*I* have seen that door into the back of the hill called Cat Bells—and besides *I* am very well acquainted with dear Mrs. Tiggy-winkle!)

FOR THE REAL LITTLE LUCIE OF NEWLANDS

FREDERICK WARNE

Published by the Penguin Group
Registered office: 80 Strand, London, WC2R 0RL
Penguin Young Readers Group, 345 Hudson Street, New York, N.Y. 10014, USA

First published 1905 by Frederick Warne
This edition with new reproductions of Beatrix Potter's book illustrations first published 2006
This edition copyright © Frederick Warne & Co. 2006
Reissued 2016
New reproductions of Beatrix Potter's book illustrations copyright © Frederick Warne & Co. 2002
Original copyright in text and illustrations © Frederick Warne & Co., 1905

Manufactured in China

Special Markets ISBN 978-0-241-29836-7